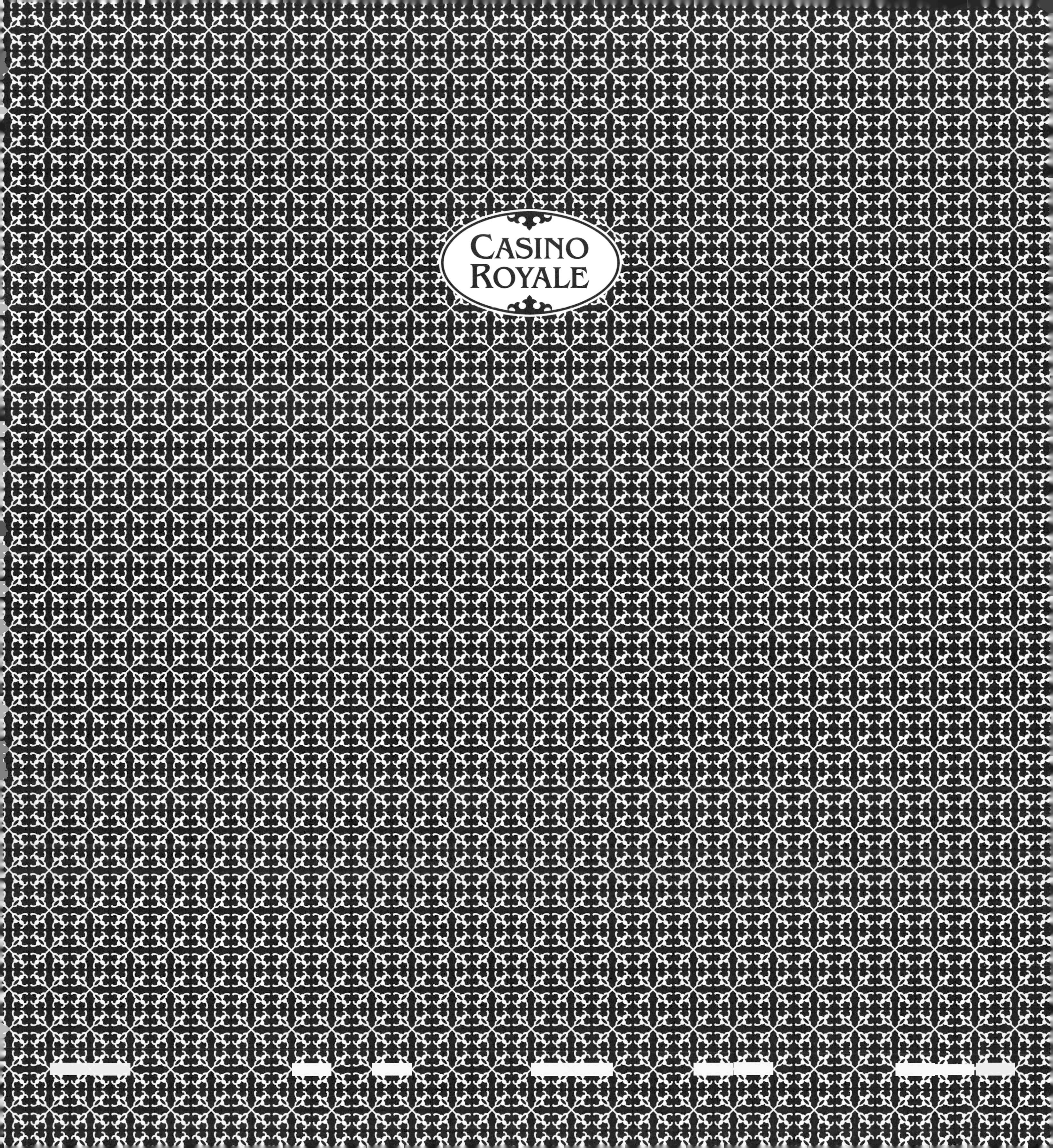
CASINO
ROYALE

BOND ON SET

GREG WILLIAMS

FILMING 007
CASINO ROYALE

LONDON, NEW YORK, MUNICH,
MELBOURNE, and DELHI

Art Direction / Design Mike Bone
Senior Editor Alastair Dougall
Designer Lauren Egan
Brand Manager Lisa Lanzarini
Publishing Manager Simon Beecroft
Category Publisher Alex Allan
Production Rochelle Talary
DTP Designer Hanna Ländin
Color retouching Hanna Ländin, Peter Pawsey

First American Edition, 2006
06 07 08 09 10 10 9 8 7 6 5 4 3 2 1

Published in the United States by DK Publishing, Inc.
375 Hudson Street, New York, New York 10014

Published in Great Britain by Dorling Kindersley Limited.

A catalog record for this book is available from the Library
of Congress.

ISBN-13: 978-0-75662-272-5
ISBN-10: 0-7566-2272-7

Hi-res workflow proofed by Wyndeham Icon Limited
Printed and bound in Mexico by R R Donnelley

Discover more at
www.dk.com

FOREWORD

Michael G. Wilson
Barbara Broccoli

The taking of photographs for *Bond on Set*, cannot be done by a photographer acting alone; it requires the cooperation of several people. You cannot even get near a film set without the permission of the producers and the director. And once there, you can only stay if the actors and assistant directors allow it. The photographer must earn the respect and trust of each of these persons to get effective pictures. It takes a special person to earn that trust – a person that is not only respected for his technical and artistic talent, but is also trusted to show what goes on behind the scenes with sensitivity, honesty, and integrity. Greg is one of the few photographers to have earned such trust and respect.

Greg worked on the set of the last Bond film, *Die Another Day*, and produced a wonderful book of images. Thus, it was no problem convincing us to come back for a second time. But the biggest challenge for Greg was how to approach the introduction of a new Bond actor and to capture the shift in style that we wanted to bring to the series.

When the original producers Cubby Broccoli and Harry Saltzman acquired the Bond film rights from Ian Fleming in 1962, the rights to *Casino Royale*, the first novel to introduce the Bond character, were not available. A Bond spoof was made from the novel in 1968, but it was not until the late 1990s that we were able to obtain the film rights for *Casino Royale*.

We set out to make *Casino Royale* as it should have been made originally, in a more realistic style than the immediate past Bond films. In tone and atmosphere the film was to be like the classic Bond films such as *Dr. No* and *From Russia With Love*. Greg had to reflect this change in his pictures. He prepared by reading the script and meeting with the producers and the director, Martin Campbell.

But all would have been for naught if Greg had not gained the confidence of the new James Bond. Daniel Craig is among the most gifted actors of his generation. He has built his career slowly, choosing his roles carefully and working with top directors. Becoming Bond was a sea-change in his life. A very private person, he realized he would suddenly be thrust into the media spotlight. Only a person of Greg's reputation and capability could have gained Daniel's trust to photograph some of his most private moments.

Needless to say, Greg won the confidence of us all and has created a wonderful book that offers the world a look behind the scenes of *Casino Royale* and the private world of those who live and work in it.

January 12, 2006: Stoke Poges, England
Daniel Craig practices handling various types of guns on the firing range.

October 10, 2005: London, England
A private moment before going to meet the worldwide media for the first time as 007.

ROLL
B
43
DIR:

NO ROYALE
SCENE
TAKE
4G
3
PANAVISION
B
TIN CAMPBELL
MÉHEUX BSC
FEB '06

February 6, 2006: Barrandov Studios, Prague, Czech Republic
Enemy agent Fisher (Daud Shah) becomes James Bond's first-ever kill.

February 6, 2006: Prague, Czech Republic
Daniel Craig and his stunt double, Ben Cooke, between takes during the fight sequence.

NISSAN
RM 8652

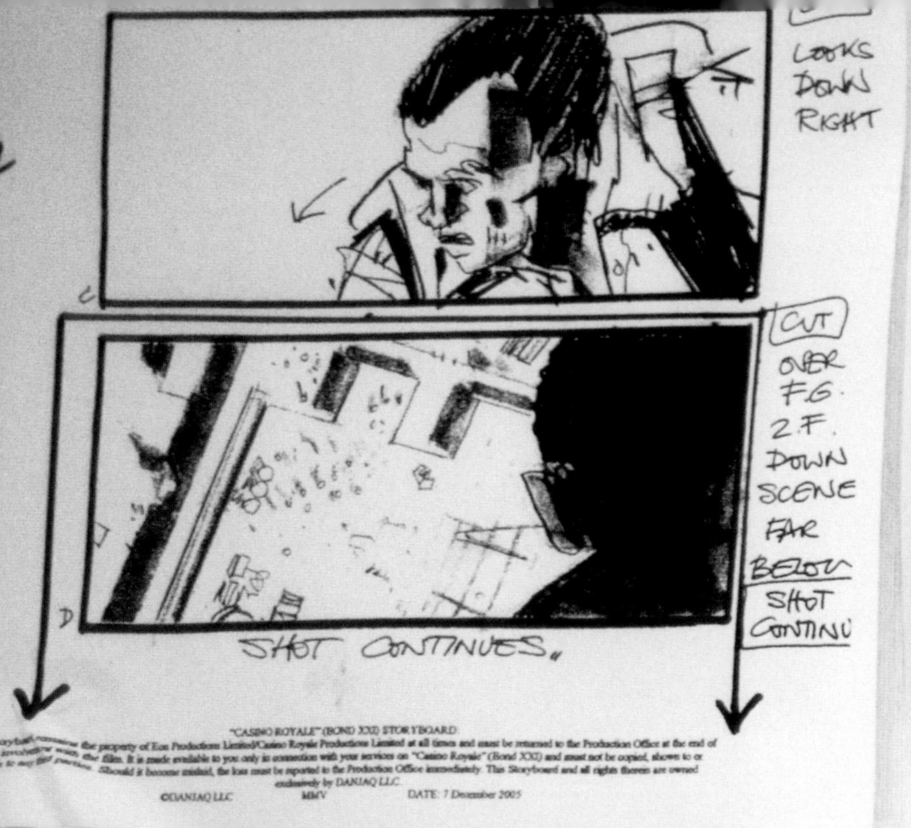

LOOKS DOWN RIGHT
C
CUT
OVER F.G. 2.F. DOWN SCENE FAR BELOW
D
SHOT CONTINUES..
SHOT CONTINU
"CASINO ROYALE" (BOND XXI) STORYBOARD:
©DANJAQ LLC
MMV
DATE: 7 December 2005

176
BOND: "You've had your ten!"
C
CUT
WIDER
FROM F.G. BOND
177
T.F. THROWS GUN –
BOND REACHES – CATCHES IT
"CASINO ROYALE" (BOND XXI) STORYBOARD:
This storyboard remains the property of Eon Productions Limited/Casino Royale Productions Limited at all times and must be returned to the Production Office at the end of your involvement with the film. It is made available to you only in connection with your services on "Casino Royale" (Bond XXI) and must not be copied, shown to or given to any third parties. Should it become mislaid, the loss must be reported to the Production Office immediately. This Storyboard and all rights therein are owned exclusively by DANJAQ LLC.
©DANJAQ LLC
MMV
DATE: 7 December 2005

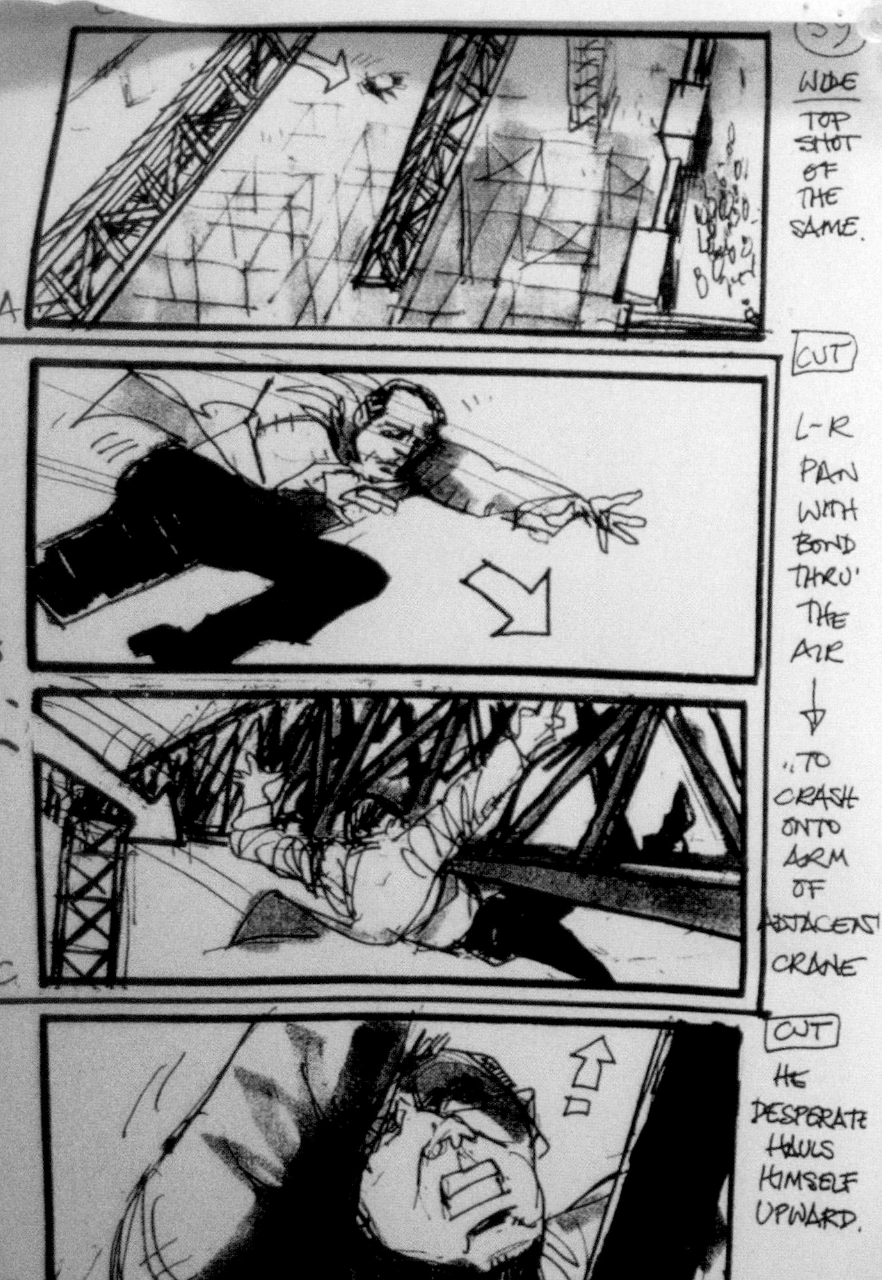

WIDE
TOP SHOT OF THE SAME.
A
CUT
L-R PAN WITH BOND THRU' THE AIR
B
..TO CRASH ONTO ARM OF ADJACENT CRANE
C.
CUT
HE DESPERATE HAULS HIMSELF UPWARD.
D
CUT
"CASINO ROYALE" (BOND XXI) STORYBOARD:

60
ANGLE ON SLOPING ROOFS.
T.F. SLIDES DOWN THEN LEAPS TO TH NE
CONSTRUCTION SITE
216
A
217
B
218
C

"CASINO ROYALE" (BOND XXI) STORYBOARD
184
ANGLE ON SCENE
CUT
C.U. Z.F.
BY GUN
HE DROPS
CONSTRUCTION SITE
61
GANG OF SECURITY MEN RUN TO CAM
ALL ONE SHOT
T.F. DROPS IN FRONT OF THEM
CUT
BACK TO BOND.
HE LEAPS OF CRANE #2 AND..
CUT
LANDS
SHOT
CUT
HE RUN TO C.U AND EXITS R-L
CUT
62
PREVIOUS CONT.
BOND TUMBLES OF STRUCTURE
FALLS HEAVILY ONTO ROOF.
223
CUT
224
C.U. HE REARS UP INTO SHOT –
EXITS L-R
CUT
BACK TO T.F.
225
TOP SHOT
HE RUNS TO STAIRWELL, LEAPS DOWN TO LANDING
CUT

March 3, 2006: Nassau, Bahamas (for Madagascar)
Sébastien Foucan, the real-life co-founder of Parkour (free running), takes a death-defying leap as Mollaka, a terrorist bomber attempting to evade 007.

Next page: Sébastien Foucan.

VERIFICAT
CAB

March 16, 2006: Nassau, Bahamas
Above: Daniel Craig checks his script in his trailer.
Opposite: Daniel Craig wearing a stunt harness
required for a sequence filmed at dangerous
heights during the construction-site chase.

March 16, 2006: Nassau, Bahamas (for Madagascar)
The crew consults during shooting of the construction-site chase. From left: Second Unit 1st Assistant Director Terry Madden, Second Unit Director and DOP Alexander Witt, Director Martin Campbell.

ARVEY MUDD
ALUMNI

R-11
GU156

March 17, 2006: Nassau, Bahamas (for Madagascar)
Sébastien Foucan's stunt double leaps onto a crane.

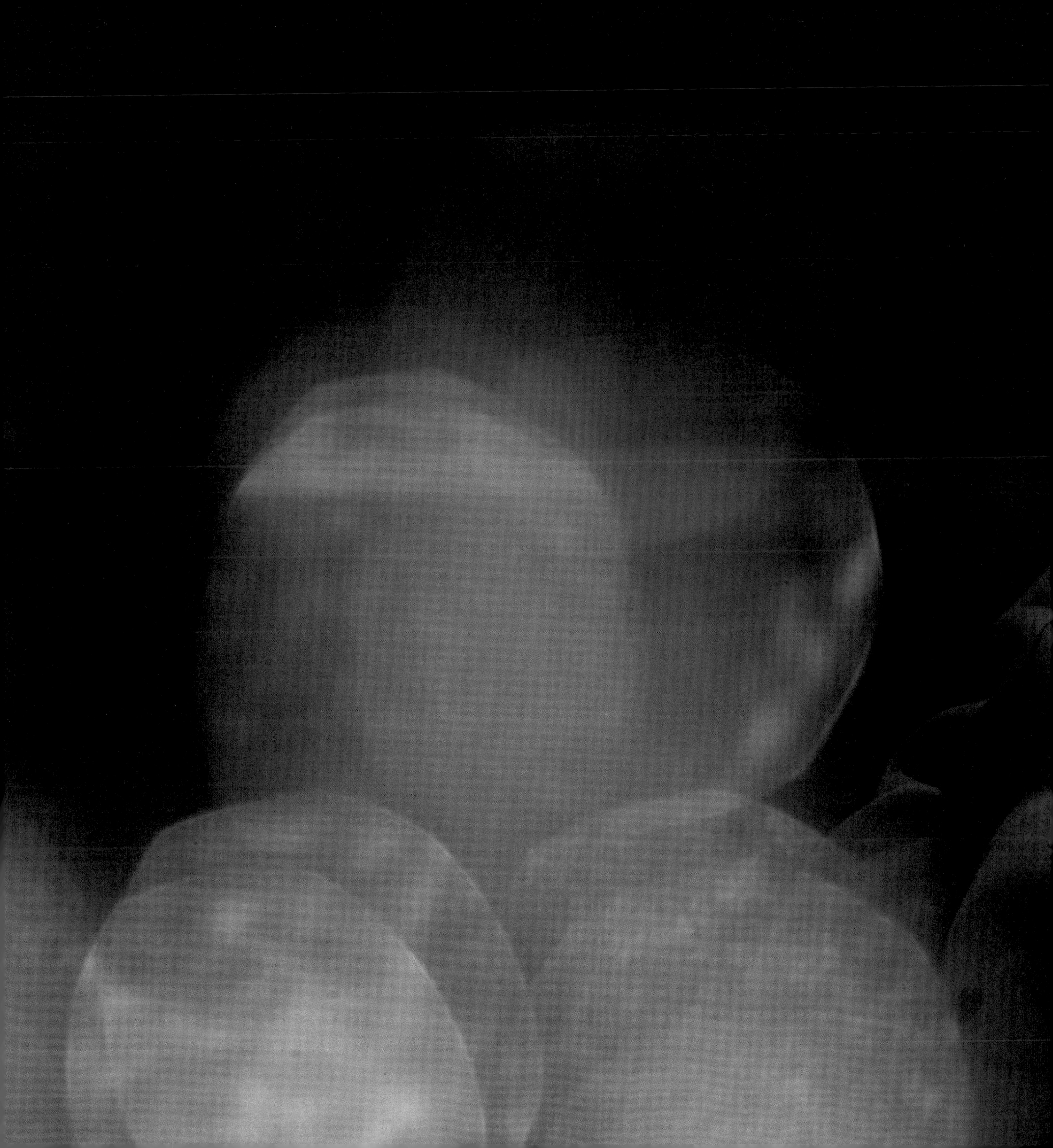

OMEN ART DEPARTMENT PRAHA 2005

February 10, 2006: Prague, Czech Republic
Art department preparing "London by night" — as seen through the window of M's office at MI6.

February 14, 2006: Prague, Czech Republic
Daniel Craig on the set of M's London apartment.

Next page: Ivana Milicevic (as Valenka) with underwater camera crew.

HYDROFLEX

March 14, 2006: Nassau, Bahamas
Bond's first glimpse of the beautiful Solange (Caterina Murino), riding her horse along the beach.

March 3, 2006: Nassau, Bahamas
Solange (Caterina Murino) with her husband, Dimitrios (Simon Abkarian), at the One and Only Ocean Club.

March 4, 2006: Nassau, Bahamas
Caterina Murino (as Solange) relaxes between takes during the shooting of her love scene with 007.

May 25, 2006: Karlovy Vary, Czech Republic (for Montenegro)
Bond walks through the Casino Royale.

April 5, 2006: Prague, Czech Republic (for Montenegro)
Director Martin Campbell works through a complex gambling scene set in Casino Royale's Salon Privé. Shooting the sequence took 15 days. This is the first day.

April 5, 2006: Prague, Czech Republic
Mads Mikkelsen: becoming Le Chiffre.

April 12, 2006: Prague, Czech Republic (for Montenegro)
Between takes of the Salon Privé poker game (from left): Jeffrey Wright (as Bond's ally, CIA agent Felix Leiter), ADE (as Infante, a gambler), and 60's supermodel Veruschka (as gambling heiress Gräfin Von Wallenstein).

DEALER
ROYALE

April 3, 2006: Prague, Czech Republic (for Montenegro)
Eva Green (as Vesper Lynd) runs through the action with her stunt double, Nikki Berwick, during filming of the fight in the stairwell.

April 3, 2006: Prague, Czech Republic (for Montenegro)
Obanno's lieutenant (Michael Offei) with his own life-size dummy, which Bond throws over railings during the stairwell fight.

April 4, 2006: Prague, Czech Republic (for Montenegro)
Isaach de Bankole as the brutal Obanno, who attacks 007 with a machete in the stairwell fight.

April 25, 2006: Prague, Czech Republic (for Montenegro)
Bond comforts Vesper as she tries to wash blood from her fingernails, following the harrowing stairwell fight.

May 26, 2006: Karlovy Vary, Czech Republic
Eva Green relaxes by playing the piano while waiting for the crew to set up a scene. The piano was in the restaurant where the Hotel Splendide celebration was filmed.

May 23, 2006: Karlovy Vary, Czech Republic (for Montenegro)
Eva Green (as Vesper) makes a spectacular entrance in the restaurant of the Hotel Splendide.

April 27, 2006: Prague, Czech Republic (for Montenegro)
Daniel Craig is made up to show injuries Bond suffers in a car crash prior to his capture by Le Chiffre.

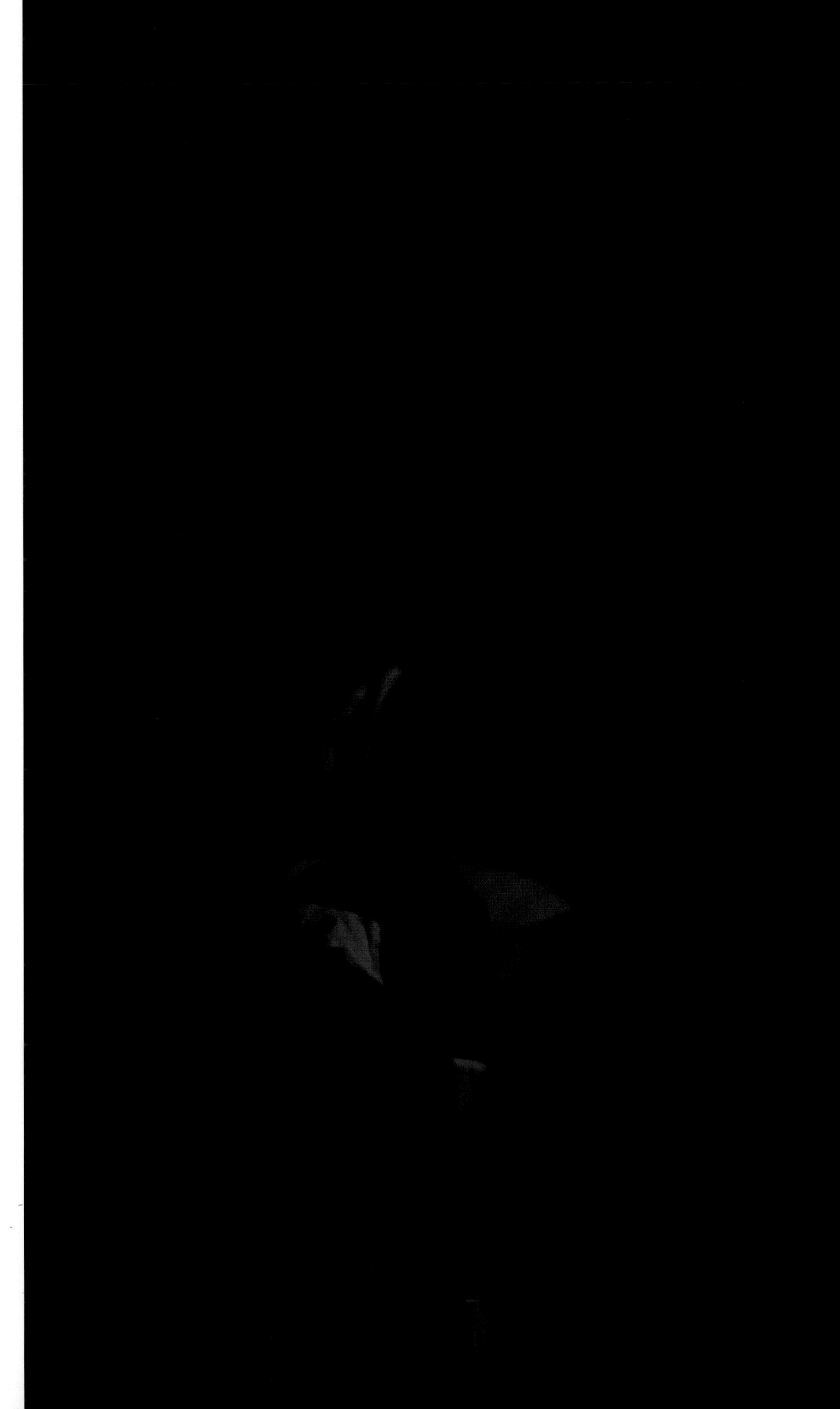

April 27, 2006: Czech Republic (for Montenegro)
Between takes on the torture scene; Le Chiffre's henchmen look on.

April 28, 2006: Prague, Czech Republic (for Montenegro)
Mads Mikkelsen contemplates the final confrontation scene between Bond and Le Chiffre.

May 31, 2006: Villa Balbianello, Italy
Above: Eva Green jokes with the photographer between takes at the Villa Balbianello during the Bond convalescence scenes.
Opposite: rest and recuperation for Vesper and Bond.

February 21, 2006: Nassau, Bahamas (for the Greek Islands)
First Assistant Director Bruce Moriarty leads the crew out of the sea, having completed shooting the beach love scene between Bond and Vesper.

Pages 110 — 21:
All photographed in the Bahamas.

June 7, 2006: Venice, Italy
Eva Green aboard the Spirit 54 Yacht on the Grand Canal.

June 3, 2006: Venice, Italy
Chloe Meddings, Hannah Brown, Eva Green, and crew members protect their ears against the crack of gunfire.

June 3, 2006: Venice, Italy
Vesper (Eva Green) is threatened by
the assassin Gettler (Richard Sammel).

June 29, 2006: 007 Stage, Pinewood, England (for the Grand Canal, Venice)
Bond tries to rescue Vesper as the derelict villa collapses into the canal.

May 30, 2006: Villa Gaeta, Lake Como, Italy
Bond in the final scene of *Casino Royale*.

Daniel Craig and Greg Williams in conversation
July 27, 2006: London

Cover

Cover
February 9, 2006: Prague

DC: I've got band-aid all over my hands because I was hitting things. [About the iris-spinning shooting shot] This was one of those classic Bond moments when you think, "Oh, we're going to have to deal with this now, are we?" I'm just pleased with the shape we created in the end, especially with this photograph, because it's very solid and that was the important thing.

We have a much more modern idea of how the police shoot guns nowadays. All over the world, officers hold a gun with two hands. That's how you aim and keep the gun steady. I practiced as hard as I could to shoot in as solid a position as possible, so it genuinely looked like an attempt at shooting somebody as opposed to just creating a shape.

Personally, all I see when I see that image is "Ow!" because those four days filming the bathroom fight really hurt!

Page 012

Page 012
October 10, 2005: London

DC: It was the day before we left to do the press launch. There's Sally my agent. I'm probably clinging on to Satsuki [Daniel's girlfriend] for dear life. It's a very private moment.

Pages 016 & 017

Pages 016 & 017
February 6, 2006: Prague

GW: This was a few days of completely battering yourself!

DC: We're in a bathroom with tiled walls. We're smashing glass. And we've got guns in our hands. I had to keep smashing my hand against one of these pictures and my hand just came up like a balloon. There wasn't an awful lot we could do about that. We just had to carry on.

Page 020

Page 020
February 6, 2006: Prague

GW: You look exhausted.

DC: Yeah, we all were. Ben Cooke [the stuntman] did a huge amount. He was a great double for me, which did make things easier.

Pages 022 & 023

Page 026

Page 033

Pages 022 & 023
March 17, 2006: Bahamas

DC: Who's winning — that's the question!

GW: I remember you falling over.

DC: What — in front of the car?

GW: Yup, you only just sat up quick enough.

DC: Yeah, I felt it go past my head. I was in a lot of pain throughout this scene. I'd done my Achilles tendon and whenever I had to do a running sequence it was agony. When I look at these shots of me running, I can tell I'm carrying an injury. That was frustrating as I kept having to go to the monitor and, if it didn't look right, we had to go back and do it again. Look how chilled out Sébastien [the bomber] is here. And I'm like...!!

GW: How did you hurt your Achilles?

DC: By falling in front of another car.

Page 026
March 3, 2006: Bahamas

DC: Sébastien is really jumping there, isn't he?

GW: Yup, there is a wire there, but it's not tight.

DC: What is it there for then?

GW: I think it's there for the insurance people.

DC: By the end he could stand on a 1-foot square on top of a 200 foot crane. Not that he was afraid of heights, but we were really high up and I think it was new stuff even for him.

Page 033
March 16, 2006: Bahamas

DC: That's me in my harness, which I wanted to burn at the end of the film but they wouldn't let me because they wanted to use it again.

GW: Didn't you have a fitting for it?

DC: Yes, but I put on quite a lot of weight working out in the gym between the time I had it fitted and the time I got a chance to wear it. So it was always very tight. The harness needs to be very tight and snug, but in the Bahamas the weather was boiling and I had to wear it with padding on top and a costume on top of that.

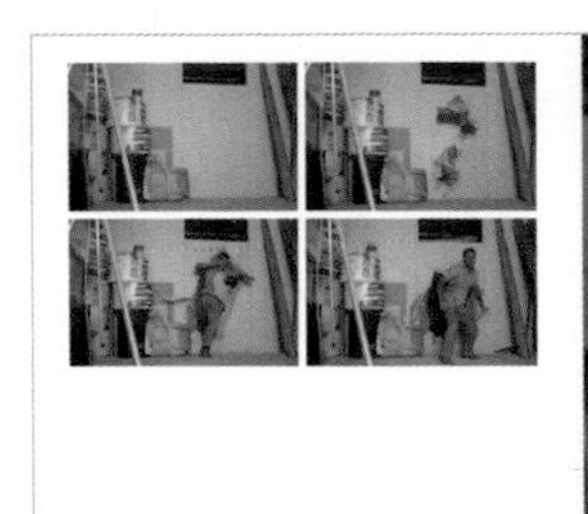

Pages 038 & 039

Page 064

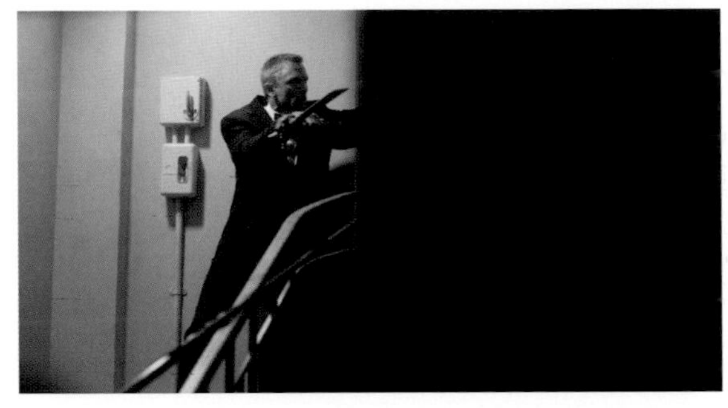

Page 076

Page 086

Pages 038 & 039
March 17, 2006: Bahamas

DC: Bashing through a wall. They score a plaster wall with a razor and I bash through it.

Page 064
February 7, 2006: Prague

GW: This was the day after you'd finished the fight scene in the toilets.

DC: That would explain why I'm fast asleep.

Page 076
April 3, 2006: Prague

DC: Doing a fight sequence in a stairwell is about as awkward as it can get. Thankfully, some of the walls and banisters were padded, so we were able to throw ourselves around a bit, but it was still quite dangerous. Ben, my stunt double, really hurt himself throwing himself down the stairs. They say that stuntmen make falling down the stairs look easy but you ask a stuntman what it feels like and he'll tell you, "It feels like falling down the stairs!"

Page 086
April 4, 2006: Prague

GW: During shooting of the stairwell fight, you got hit in the eye, didn't you?

DC: Yeah, I did.

GW: I remember — you had to cover it up the next day.

DC: We finished the fight and went straight into the casino and I had to do most of the casino scenes with a black eye because I got head-butted. You can't blame him. I was trying to choke him.

Page 094

Pages 128 & 129

Page 132

Page 094
May 23, 2006: Karlovy Vary, Czech Republic

DC: There's one of the cars I broke. Adam my stunt driver broke three. He turned two over then just wrecked the other one. I burned the clutch out on one of them the other day.

GW: On a DBS?

DC: Oh completely. Hands up — I broke it. It was the last day of shooting down at Dunsfold, where the action unit was filming. I took the car to about 150 down the road. Trouble was, I put the brakes on too soon and took it down to second too quickly. I did it once and it seemed to like it OK. And I tried to do it again and it didn't like it. Smoke started to come out of the dashboard.

Pages 128 & 129
June 29, 2006: Venice

GW: Tell me about being in the biggest Jacuzzi on earth.

DC: You can't imagine what an amazing piece of engineering that Venice house set was. They sank a house 7,8,9 times a day into 20 feet of water, dragged it out and did it again. The lift cage fell over and stuff fell all over the place. It's really spectacular.

Page 132
May 30, 2006: Lake Como, Italy

GW: In the script, you were supposed to shoot Mr White with a handgun. How come you used this monster?

DC: In this scene I shoot someone in the knee. You don't see me do it, but you see his knee exploding. I could have shot him from 20 yards away with a handgun but I just thought: Bond's not in that mood. He's in the mood to hurt somebody. This is an assault weapon with a silencer on it and from 20 or 30 yards it's absolutely deadly. You could hit him anywhere on the body with it. Plus the fact it's BIG.

This is the last scene in the movie and I wanted to show that Bond means business. We don't know if he kills this guy. We certainly suspect that he is going to extract some information from him.

19 89
CR

CASINO ROYALE
007
21
MARTIN CAMPBELL

CAST & CREW

James Bond	DANIEL CRAIG
Vesper Lynd	EVA GREEN
Le Chiffre	MADS MIKKELSEN
M	JUDI DENCH
Felix Leiter	JEFFREY WRIGHT
Mathis	GIANCARLO GIANNINI
Solange	CATERINA MURINO
Dimitrios	SIMON ABKARIAN
Obanno	ISAACH DE BANKOLE
Mr. White	JESPER CHRISTENSEN
Valenka	IVANA MILICEVIC
Villiers	TOBIAS MENZIES
Carlos	CLAUDIO SANTAMARIA
Mollaka	SÉBASTIEN FOUCAN
Dryden	MALCOLM SINCLAIR
John Bliss	CON O'NEILL
Gettler	RICHARD SAMMEL
Banker Mendel	LUDGER PISTOR
Carter	JOSEPH MILLSON
Fisher	DAUD SHAH
Kratt	CLEMENS SCHICK
Leo	EMMANUEL AVENA
Stockbroker	TOM CHADBON
Obanno's Lieutenant	MICHAEL OFFEI

CASINO ROYALE PLAYERS

Infante	ADE
Tomelli	URBANO BARBERINI
Madame Wu	TSAI CHIN
Gallardo	CHARLIE LEVI LEROY
Kaminofsky	LAZAR RISTOVSKI
Fukutu	TOM SO
Gräfin Von Wallenstein	VERUSCHKA

Michael G Wilson	Producer
Barbara Broccoli	Producer
Martin Campbell	Director
Neal Purvis	Writer
Robert Wade	Writer
Paul Haggis	Writer
Anthony Waye	Executive Producer
Callum McDougall	Executive Producer
Andrew Noakes	Associate Producer
David Wilson	Assistant Producer
Peter Lamont	Production Designer
Phil Méheux BSC	Director Of Photography / Main Unit
Stuart Baird	Editor
Lindy Hemming	Costume Designer
David Arnold	Composer
Alexander Witt	2nd Unit Director & DOP
Gary Powell	Stunt Co-ordinator
Chris Corbould	Special Effects & Miniature Effects Supervisor
Debbie McWilliams	Casting Director
Steve Begg	Visual Effects & Miniature Supervisor
Danny Kleinman	Main Title Designer
Bruce Moriarty	1st Assistant Director / Main Unit
Roger Pearce	Camera Operator / Main Unit
Jaromír Šedina	B Camera Operator / Main Unit
Chris Munro	Sound Mixer
Jean Bourne	Script Supervisor
Toby Hefferman	2nd AD / Main Unit
Ben Dixon	2nd AD / Main unit
Simon Lamont	Supervising Art Director
Simon Wakefield	Set Decorator
Lee Sandales	Set Decorator
Ty Teiger	Property Master
Steve Bohan	Construction Manager
Martin Asbury	Storyboard Artist
Jeremy Johns	Production Supervisor
Jasmina Torbati	Production Manager (CZ)
Chris Brock	Production Manager (BHS & Italy)
Janine Modder	Production Manager (UK)
Pavel Mrkous	Location Manager (CZ)
Alex Gladstone	Location Manager (BHS)
Robin Higgs	Location Manager (UK)
Steve Harvey	Location Manager (UK)
Peter Notley	SFX Floor Supervisor / Main Unit
Ian Lowe	SFX Floor Supervisor / 2nd Unit
Eddie Knight	Gaffer
Stewart Monteith	Best Boy (CZ & BHS)
Paul Engelen	Make Up Supervisor
Christine Blundell	Hairdressing Supervisor
Dan Grace	Costume Supervisor
Terry Madden	1st Assistant Director / 2nd Unit
Terry Bamber	Production Manager / 2nd Unit
Clive Jackson	Camera Operator / 2nd Unit
Lori Wyant	Script Supervisor / 2nd Unit (CZ & BHS)
Anne Bennett	Director of Marketing
Keith Snelgrove	Director of Product Placement
Linda Gamble	Unit Publicist / Main Unit
Katherine McCormack	Unit Publicist / 2nd Unit
Jay Maidment	Stills Photographer / Main Unit
Susie Allnutt	Stills Photographer / 2nd Unit
Kevin Herd	Workshop Supervisor
Paul Knowles	Workshop Supervisor
Roy Quinn	Workshop Supervisor
Tom Murtagh	Workshop Supervisor

A UK — Czech — German — US Co-Production

A Stillking — Casino Royale Productions Ltd — Casino Royale US, LLC — Babelsberg Film Co-Production

WITH THANKS

Greg Williams
NY, August 2006

A huge thank you to Michael G. Wilson and Barbara Broccoli for making me feel so totally welcome in your extended Bond family and for your kind foreword to this book. To Daniel Craig, thank you so much for allowing me to be your shadow over the last year and for all your encouragement and enthusiasm on this and every shoot we have done together. Thanks also to Satsuki Mitchell, Laura Aron and Sally Long-Innes.

To Martin Campbell, thank you for giving me such unrestricted access to your set.

To Anne Bennett, one of the most important and supportive people I have met in my career, thank you for putting so much faith in me, yet again. Many thanks also to your entire marketing and publicity department, in particular Katherine McCormack and Jenni McMurrie. At Danjaq, many thanks to Keith Snelgrove.

Thank you to Jay Maidment, for letting me shoot your set-up of the cast and crew photo.

To Mike Bone, my favorite designer, I cannot thank you enough for overseeing the entire creation of this book. Thanks to Alex Allan, Alastair Dougall and Lisa Lanzarini at Dorling Kindersley.

Thank you to the Publicity and Marketing departments at Sony.

Thanks to Brenda Brown, Matthew Moneypenny, Stephen Mayes, Gina Liberto and Cybele Sandy at Art and Commerce.

To Andrzej Michalski at Concrete Media, Joe Puleio at Digital Fusion, Steve Jackson and Chris Ellis — thank you all for your hard work.

From the Cast and Crew, there are too many people to thank in person and I'll only forget someone, so instead I will just say a massive thanks for everyone's help and friendship throughout this project. Many of you were absolutely essential to the book's creation. You know who you are. Thank you!

Finally, love and thanks to my wife Sarah for all your love and support.

JAMES BOND WILL BE BACK...